This **rising moon** book belongs to

_____

A Day With NO CRAYONS

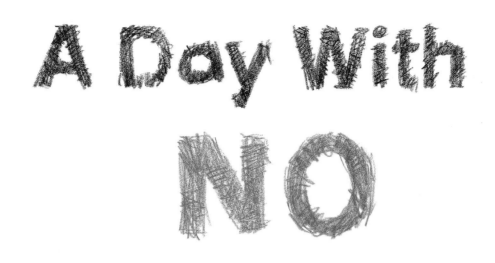

By Elizabeth Rusch

Illustrated by Chad Cameron

rising moon

www.risingmoonbooks.com

Composed in the United States of America
Printed in Malaysia

Edited by Theresa Howell
Designed by Sunny H. Yang

FIRST IMPRESSION 2007
ISBN 13: 978-0-87358-910-9
ISBN 10: 0-87358-910-6

Library of Congress Cataloging-in-Publication Data

Rusch, Elizabeth.
A day with no crayons / by Elizabeth Rusch ; illustrated by Chad Cameron.
p. cm.
Summary: A little girl discovers all sorts of artistic possibilities when she has to go a day without crayons.
ISBN-13: 978-0-87358-910-9 (hardcover)
ISBN-10: 0-87358-910-6 (hardcover)
[1. Artists--Fiction. 2. Color--Fiction. 3. Crayons--Fiction.] I. Cameron, Chad, ill. II. Title.
PZ7.R8932Day 2007
2006019608

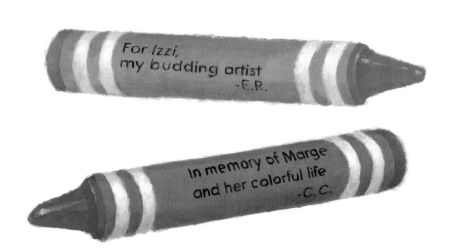

For Izzi,
my budding artist
-E.R.

In memory of Marge
and her colorful life
-C.C.

Liza loved her crayons. She treasured turquoise,
adored apricot, and flipped over fuchsia.
In fact, coloring made Liza feel tickle-me-pink.

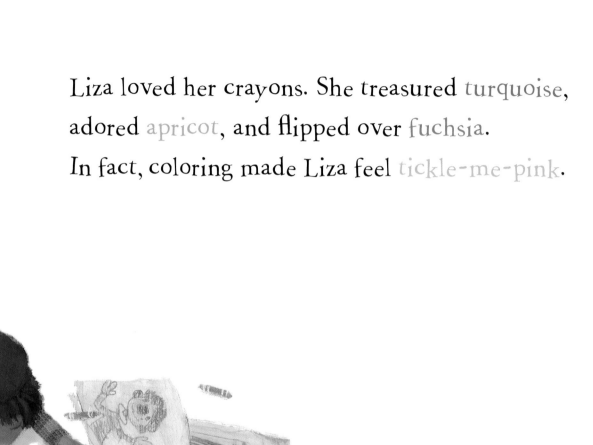

Every day, Liza filled her coloring books
with aquamarine oceans, royal purple
plums, and screamin' green dragons.
She papered the walls of her room,
the hallway, and the bathroom with
the bright, neat pages.

Then one day, Liza ran out of paper. Her coloring books were all full, and there wasn't a single sheet of blank paper left.

Liza paced her room, unsure of what to do...

...until she discovered, right in front of her, one blank wall.

"What on earth are you doing?"
her mother cried.

"Coloring," said Liza.

"Coloring? Your walls?"
her mother exclaimed.

She snatched up Liza's crayon bucket:
"No more crayons for you today."

"No crayons!" Liza cried.
"A whole day with no crayons?"

Liza shuffled to the bathroom,
feeling blue—midnight blue, in fact.

"A day with no crayons?"
she grumbled.

She gripped the toothpaste crossly,
squirting a blue-green streak across
the sink.

"Now look at the mess I've made,"
she mumbled, smearing it toward
the drain.

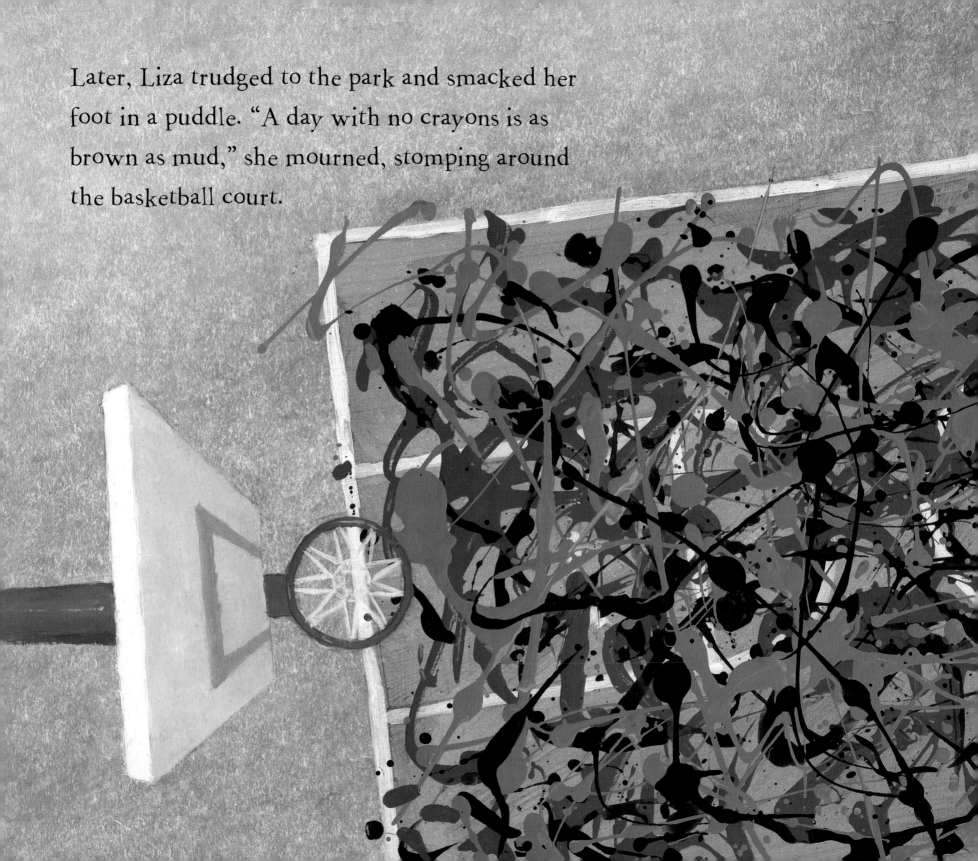

Later, Liza trudged to the park and smacked her foot in a puddle. "A day with no crayons is as brown as mud," she mourned, stomping around the basketball court.

Finally, Liza slumped to the ground and brushed her grass-stained knees.

The green wouldn't come off.

Liza leaned forward for a closer look.

"Hmm," she thought. "That's spring green and jungle green mixed."

Liza rolled over and found herself eye-to-eye with a lovely flower.

"Why, that color's not blue bell at all," she said. "It's more like cornflower."

Liza yanked a nearby dandelion and crushed it in her fist. When she opened her palm, it glowed.

"And this isn't dandelion yellow," she laughed. "It's more like laser lemon."

Liza jumped up. "It's even lovelier than laser lemon!"

Liza mashed dazzling yellow dandelions onto her cuffs. Then she squashed deep purple blackberries onto her pockets and rubbed brilliant orange tiger lilies down both legs.

Running through the park in her rainbow pants,
Liza suddenly saw color everywhere!

She dragged a muddy stick across the park, sketching a chocolate-brown tree trunk with long stretching branches.

She pressed leaves of meadow green, sea green, and forest green in the mud and squished them onto her tree until it shimmered.

She gathered flower petals and
fashioned birds that flew with
her across the park.

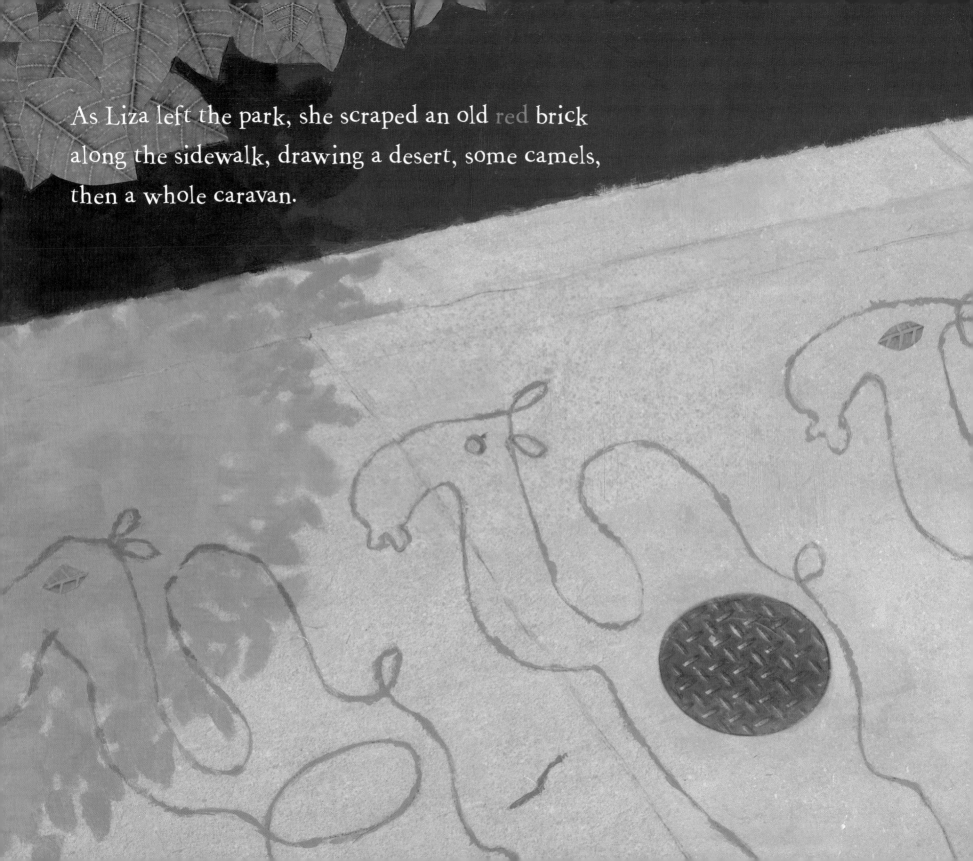

As Liza left the park, she scraped an old red brick
along the sidewalk, drawing a desert, some camels,
then a whole caravan.

Near her house, Liza gathered
gray-blue pebbles and laid
them side-by-side, until an
ocean swelled.

Up the front porch steps,
Liza scattered dandelions and
rhododendron petals until a
sunset glowed.

That night, Liza crawled in bed, arranging
her pillows around her. Outrageous orchid,
she thought. Magic maize. Wondermelon.

Her mother walked into the room,
holding Liza's crayons.

"You can have your crayons back,"
her mother said, kissing her on
the head. "If you promise not to
color on the walls."

Liza eyed the crayons her mother held
out to her. She smoothed the blankets
on her bed and considered the coloring
books spread out on the floor
around her...

"Hmm," she said.
"I think I can
go one more day
with no crayons."